FAIRY TALE CLASSICS

Cinderella

tiger tales

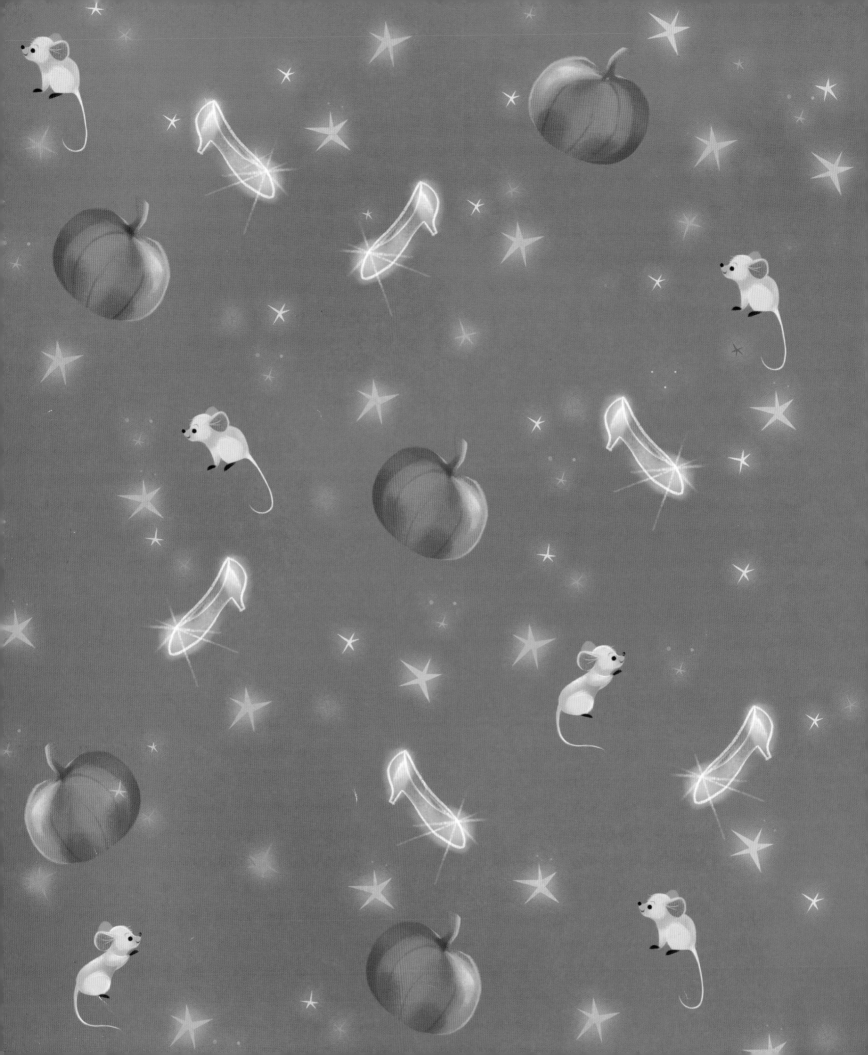

For my twirling, whirling goddaughter, Rosa ~ S.S.

To my favorite little Cinderellas, Chloe and Mia.
May you both always know that I love you very much. ~ R.R.

tiger tales

5 River Road, Suite 128, Wilton, CT 06897

Published in the United States 2018

Originally published in Great Britain 2018 by Little Tiger Press

Text adapted by Stephanie Stansbie

Text copyright © 2018 Stephanie Stansbie

Illustrations copyright © 2018 Roxanne Rainville

ISBN-13: 978-1-68010-106-5

ISBN-10: 1-68010-106-4

Printed in China

LTP/1400/2177/0318

For more insight and activities, visit us at www.tigertalesbooks.com

Cinderella

adapted by Stephanie Stansbie

Illustrated by Roxanne Rainville

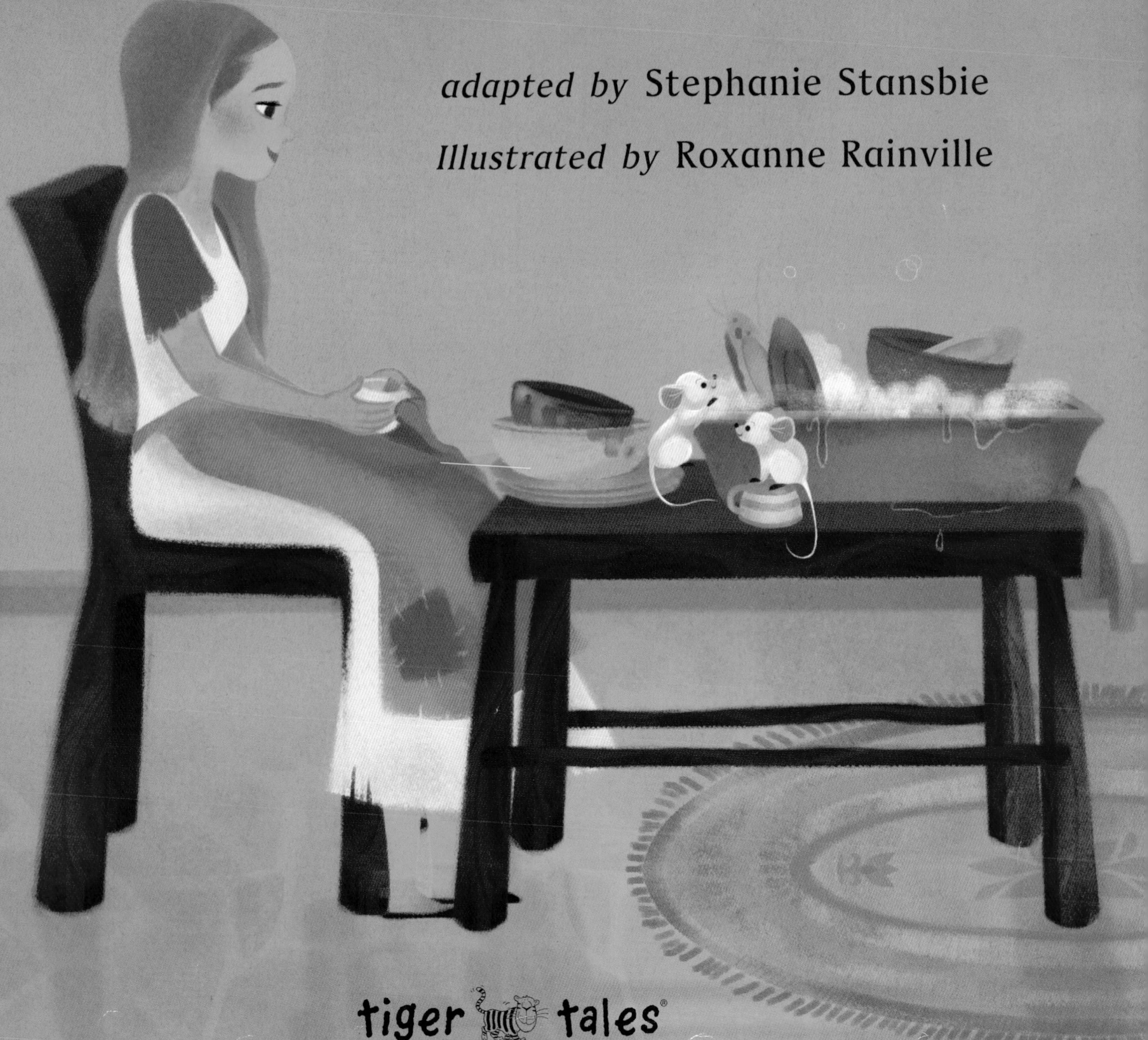

tiger tales

Ella and her father lived on their own in a big house. Ella adored dancing with her dad, twirling and whirling until her feet left the ground! She was very happy.

Then one day, her father came home with a new wife. She was incredibly beautiful, but her eyes were cold.

"This is Lady Davina," he said, "and these are her daughters, Ruby and Jade."

Ella was too stunned to speak.

Ruby and Jade cared only about clothes.
Soon they had bought so many, Ella's father
had to travel abroad to earn more money.
"Take care of my precious Ella for me," he said.

But Davina did not. She made Ella a servant and left her in rags. At night, Ella slumped by the fire with only the mice for company.

In the morning, her face was smeared with cinders.

"Here comes Smudges!" Jade jeered.

"Sooty nose!" Ruby sneered.

But if Jade was cruel and Ruby was unkind, there was nobody meaner than Lady Davina.

"From now on, we'll call you Cinderella," she snapped.

Call me what you like, thought Cinderella. *You won't change who I am.*

Don't worry, Cinders!

One day an invitation arrived from the palace:

Royal Invitation

Everybody ~ that means everybody ~ is invited to the

Prince's Ball

Dress your best and put on your dancing shoes!

Jade and Ruby were wild with excitement and squealed at Cinderella to help them into their finest gowns.

"The prince had better marry one of my daughters," Lady Davina hissed.

"I don't care about the prince," said Cinderella. "I just want to dance."

Davina and her daughters screeched with laughter.

"*You* can't go to the ball! The invitation said 'dress your best,' not 'show up in rags'!"

Ugly laughter rang in the air long after
they were gone. Cinderella was left alone in the
kitchen. Her tears traced bitter tracks through the
soot and dust on her face.

"You don't want puffy eyes for the ball," said a kindly voice.

Cinderella blinked at the strange lady before her.

"Do you like pumpkins?" the lady asked. "And mice? How about lizards?"

"Er," stammered Cinderella. "I like them very much."

"Very well," said the lady, whisking her outside and waving her wand.

Suddenly, there stood a gleaming
coach trimmed in gold, with white horses
and a driver in a lizard-green coat.

Cinderella felt a tingle in her toes, a flutter in her tummy, and a buzzing in her head.

When she looked down, she was wearing an elegant gown—with sparkling glass slippers.

"Oh, don't you look splendid!" said the lady.

"Now make sure you're home by midnight, or you'll be stuck in a pumpkin with two rodents and a reptile!"

The ball was breathtaking. Cinderella danced with a charming young man. He made her laugh and sent her twirling and whirling.

This was *not* the plan!

When she heard the chimes of midnight, she kissed her new friend on the cheek and sprinted out of the palace.

The man ran after her, but all he found was a glass shoe, which had slipped off of Cinderella's slender foot.

The following day, Davina was fuming. "You two are useless!" she screamed. "The prince didn't even look at you. He was too busy dancing with that ghastly girl!"

It's not our fault. *You* didn't spend enough on our dresses.

The next week, there was a knock
at the door, and in walked the prince.
"I'm looking for the girl who fits
this slipper," he said.

But the daughters could not squeeze their feet into the shoe.

Try harder!

Then the prince asked, "Is there anyone else?"

No!

"Only Cinderella, the maid," spat Lady Davina.

The prince frowned. "But I invited *every* person in the land," he said. "Take me to meet her."

Cinderella stepped into the gleaming glass slipper.
It fit perfectly. And when the prince brushed
the hair from her face, he saw she was his love
from the night before.

"Will you marry me?" he whispered.

"Maybe," Cinderella said. "Once I know
you better."

We told you
not to worry!

"Fair enough," said the prince. "But what about these horrible women?"

"Leave them," said Cinderella. "They only value money, so they'll never be happy."

Cinderella was right. And when her father returned from his travels, he threw them out of the house.

From then on, Cinderella lived a blissful life. And she still loved to dance, twirling and whirling, with her wonderful family.

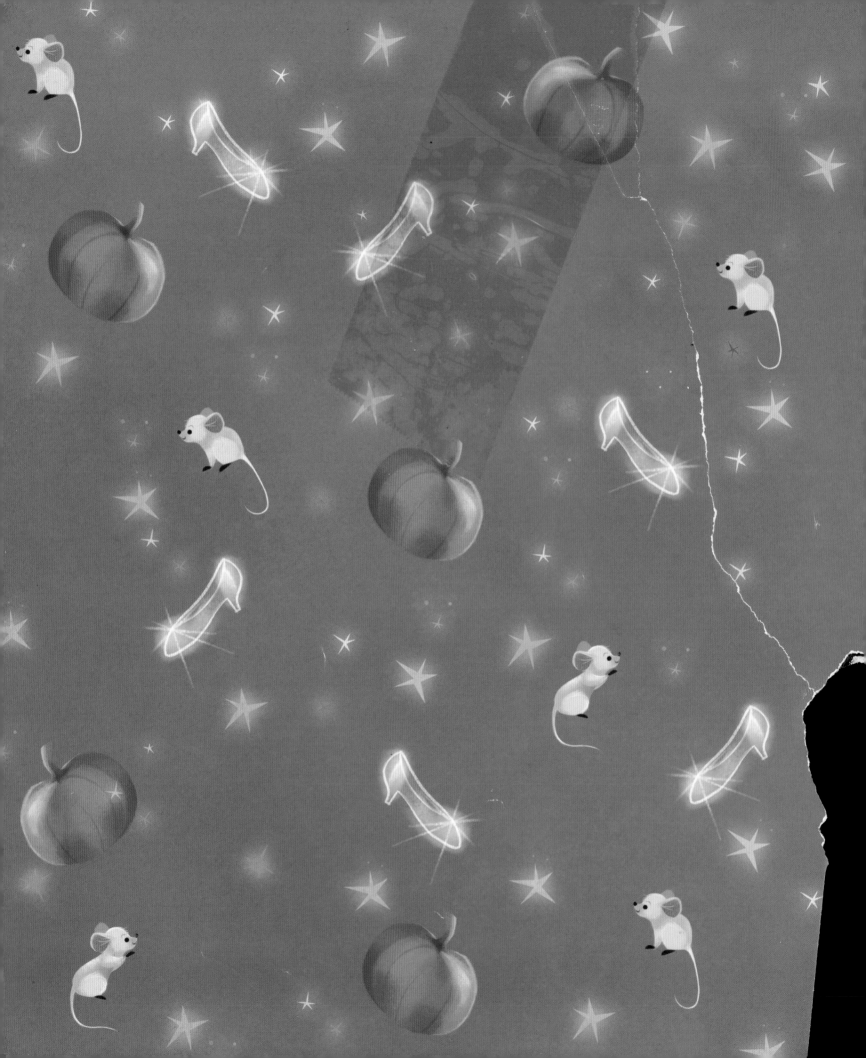

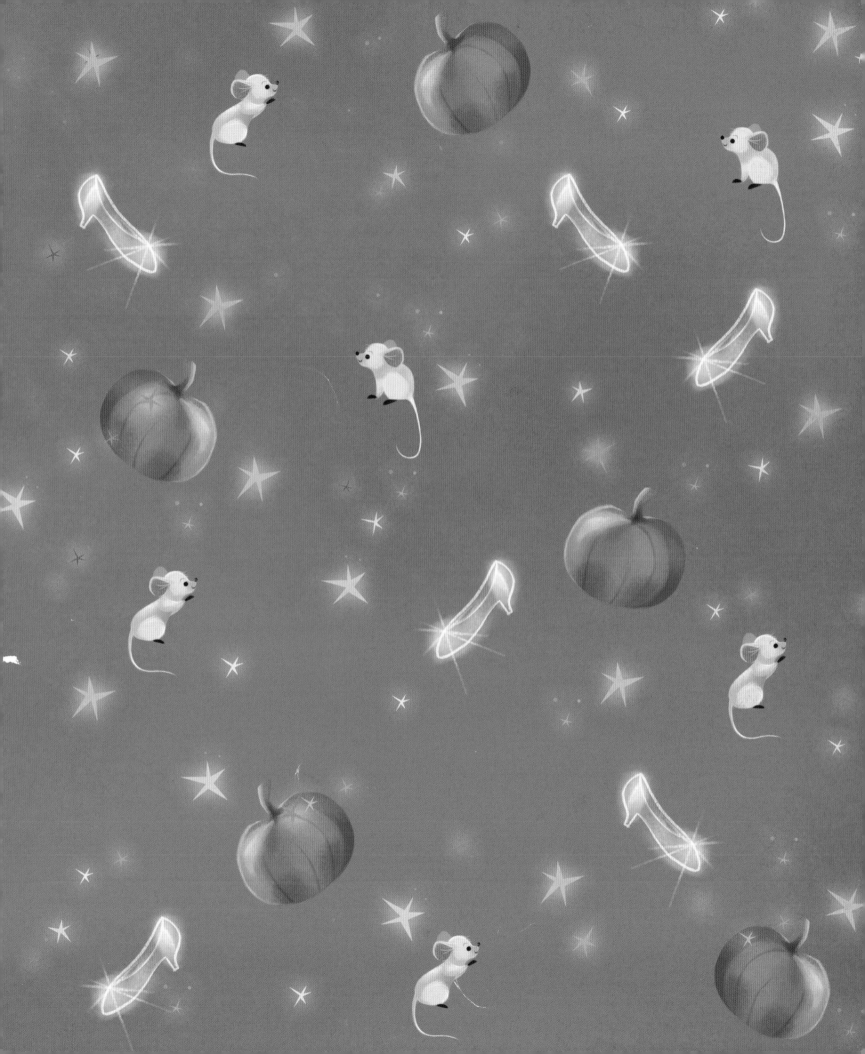

Stephanie Stansbie

Stephanie has never stopped loving fairy tales.
She has written a number of picture books, as well as a nonfiction
book called *Dinosaur*. In her spare time, she enjoys capoeira
and spending time with her family.

Roxanne Rainville

Roxanne is a freelance children's book illustrator who studied
animation, fine arts, illustration, and design in Canada. After graduating,
she worked in Montreal's gaming industry for four years before moving
back to Ontario to pursue her dream of becoming an illustrator.
She has worked on a variety of projects, from children's books to
TV shows to learning apps. She lives in the country in Ontario and
in her spare time enjoys biking, kayaking, and crafting.